Leo the Lop
Tail Three

Written by Stephen Cosgrove
Illustrated by Robin James

A Serendipity™ *Book*

PRICE STERN SLOAN

The Serendipity™ series was created by Stephen Cosgrove and Robin James.

Copyright © 2002, 1978 by Price Stern Sloan. All rights reserved.
Published by Price Stern Sloan, a division of
Penguin Putnam Books for Young Readers, New York.
345 Hudson Street, New York, NY 10014.

ISBN 0-8431-7726-8

2002 Revised Edition

2002 Printing

Dedicated to Jennifer and Julie, my two, beautiful daughters who, though now older, still get bored on cloudy days.

—Stephen

Beyond the horizon, farther than far, in the middle of the Crystal Sea, was a beautiful island called Serendipity. On this magical island, in the middle of the Forest of Dreams, protected by a wall of flowers and ferns was a glen called the Thicket. It was in the Thicket that the Serendipity bunnies lived.

In the Forest of Dreams the seasons followed Nature's order; winter, spring, summer, and fall. The branches of the trees sprouted new leaves in the spring, blossomed in the summer, and in the fall the leaves, yellow-gold, spiraled softly to the ground.

That left only the quiet time, the cold reflection of winter. The snow fell, bringing the quiet hush of winter to the forest. With each passing day, more and more snow fell until everything was covered in a soft and gentle blanket.

All of the creatures of the forest were warmly nestled in their winter beds, dreaming of the spring to come.

This was the Season of Snow.

All of the creatures, that is, except for a furry, flop-eared rabbit named Leo the Lop who was hideously bored with the long, gray winter days.

It wasn't that he didn't like winter, for he thought the season was very pretty indeed, but all of his friends, Squeakers the squirrel, Jingle Bear, and all the others had hibernated. They had gone to sleep for the winter.

Now, the only one awake, and feeling oh-so-alone, poor Leo the Lop had nothing to do!

Leo searched in vain for something to do. In the back of the bunny burrow he found an old board game and tried to play against himself but that was no fun at all. He knew the moves he was going to make before he made them.

He tried making funny faces in the mirror but he was so bored that his 'faces' didn't make him laugh at all. If anything he became even more bored, if such a thing was possible.

"There's nothing to do!" he sighed. "I am so bored."

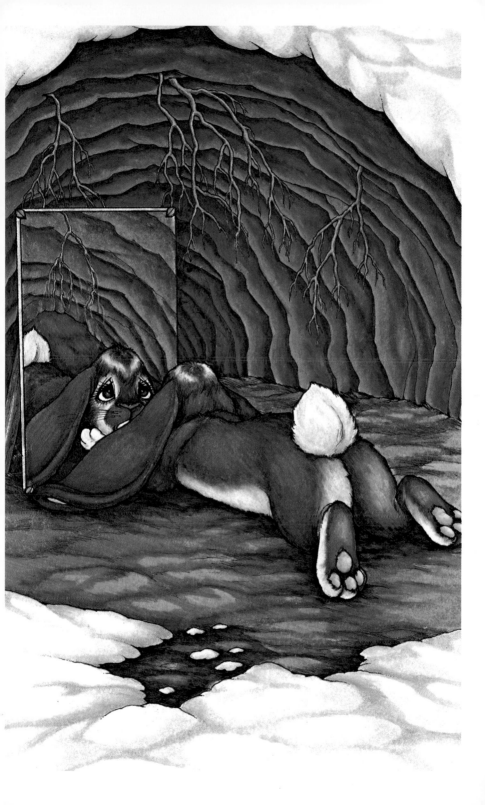

"I've been inside for such a long time," he said one morning, "the Season of Snow must be almost over. I'll bet it's almost spring. All my friends must be waking up!"

With that he wrapped himself up in his favorite plaid scarf, put on his woolen bunny mittens and dashed happily out into the snow.

"I can't wait to see Squeakers. He's probably waiting for me right now."

Happily, Leo the Lop hopped down the snow-covered Twisty Trail to the old oak tree where Squeakers lived.

When Leo got there it was very quiet and no one seemed to be up and around. He carefully climbed up until he came to the crook where a big old branch joined with the trunk of the tree. Here was the squirrel hole where his friend and his family lived. He peered inside and just could barely see Squeakers, his mom, and his dad curled up asleep.

He softly tapped on the bark of the tree. "Hey, Squeakers!" he whispered. "Squeakers wake up. Winter is almost over. Wake up and let's play!"

He waited and listened very carefully but the only thing he heard was some soft snoring and somebody mumbling in their sleep.

"He probably didn't hear me!" Leo thought.

"Squeakers!" he shouted as he pounded on the tree. "Wake up!"

There was a rumbling and a grumbling from inside. But it wasn't Squeakers. It was Squeakers' father and he was not very happy at all. In fact he was as grumpy as an old bear. Leo was so scared that he stepped back, forgetting that he was standing on the branch of the tree. Down plopped Leo the Lop into the snow below.

"What do you want?" grumbled the old squirrel, "It's only half past winter, child, it's still the Season of Snow. Why aren't you asleep?"

"There's nothing to do!" said Leo brightly. "So, I thought I'd see if Squeakers was awake so we could play."

The old squirrel looked at him in disbelief. "Go back to bed, silly bunny. You can play with Squeakers in the spring." With a yawn and a stretch he shuffled back into the warm comfort of the tree, leaving Leo alone again.

Now Leo was not one to give up easily and simply go back to his winter's bed. Besides he couldn't sleep and he wanted to play. Still bored, he began hopping down the trail with every intent of finding the hidden den where Jingle Bear was sleeping, which probably was not a good idea at all. Jingle Bear's dad was not a happy bear even in the summer.

It was quite fortunate that he found five little twitter birds instead. "Hi, birds!" he said. "I'm bored and don't have anything to do. Do you want to play?"

The twitter birds chattered coldly, "Are you kidding? It's the middle of the Season of Snow. All our waking hours must be spent looking for dried nuts and berries in the trees and bushes. We have no time for play with a silly rabbit!" And with that they flew away in a flutter of feathers.

Once again, Leo the Lop was left alone, with nothing to do!

Leo was very bored. There was nothing to do and no one to do it with if he could find something to do.

"Oh, pooh!" he grumbled.

"Pooh, who?" a voice called out.

Leo looked up and roosting in the branch was his teacher from Critter School, old Teacher Owl. "There's really no 'pooh,' sir," said Leo with a sigh. "I was bored and wanted to wake somebody up to play with. Squeakers' dad got mad and the birds are too busy. I was gonna wake up Jingle Bear but I know his dad would growl my head off, for sure. I'm bored and there's nothing to do!"

The old owl, being wise by nature, thought for a moment and then softly whooed, "Did you ever stop to think, that maybe you could play by yourself and have just as much fun? Later, come the spring, you can tell all your friends about your marvelous winter fun in the Season of Snow."

"Well, I'll try." Sighed Leo as he started to walk away. Suddenly with a smile on his fuzzy face he turned and asked brightly, "Uh, do you want to play?"

"No, Leo. Be by yourself. Trust me, you will have fun." And with that old Teacher Owl flew away leaving Leo sitting in the snow all alone.

There was still nothing to do. . .

. . .or was there?

"Well," he sighed, "I guess I've got to try to find some fun somewhere!" And try he did. He hopped up the mountain, higher and higher through the heavy snow searching and searching for something to do, but he found nothing at all, save for the top of hill.

"I'm tired of hopping through the snow," he said. "Maybe I'll just slide down the hill and go home."

He sat back on his big feet and slid quickly down the hill. "Hmmm," he thought, "that was fun. In fact that was a lot of fun! I'm gonna do it again."

With that he quickly hopped back up the hill and skied back down again! "Wheee!" he laughed, his voice echoing into the forest.

After skiing for an hour or more, Leo was becoming a master at playing by himself. "Maybe there are other things I can do alone," He laughed.

He looked around and then knelt down, scooped up some soft snow in his paws and made a snowball. He packed more and more snow onto the ball and when it was big enough he put it on the ground and began to roll it around and around. Slowly the snowball grew bigger and bigger and bigger. When it was so big that Leo could barely roll it he started another one.

He rolled another and another and finally stacked them on top of each other. With his hands and a short stick he carved the biggest snow bunny that had ever been built on the Island of Serendipity. Boy, was that fun!

Later that afternoon, Leo went back to the bunny burrow a tired, but very happy, rabbit.

He played like this for days and days. Building snow bunnies, sliding down the hills and once or twice he just laid in the snow waving his arms making funny figures.

One day as he was playing, he noticed a small green shoot peeping through the snow. He looked around and, sure enough, there were little green shoots all over the place.

"It's the beginning of spring!" he shouted gleefully.

Sure enough, Leo had been having so much fun he didn't even know that spring had sprung. As the snow slowly melted, the other creatures of the forest began to wake from their deep winters' sleep.

Leo wasn't alone anymore.

Leo the Lop spent most of the spring and part of the summer telling the other creatures about the wonderful time he had during the winter playing by himself.

And though he played with all the animals whenever he could, once and a while Leo would go off alone and play by himself.

SO, WHEN YOU'RE ALL ALONE,

AND IT SEEMS LIKE

THERE'S NOTHING TO DO

REMEMBER LEO'S LESSON. . .

. . .YOU CAN ALWAYS PLAY WITH YOU.

Serendipity™ Books

Created by
Stephen Cosgrove and Robin James

Enjoy all the delightful books in the Serendipity™ Series:

Available wherever books are sold.

PRICE STERN SLOAN